KT-497-936

The PaIN and the Great One
Cool Zone

The Pain and the Great One series
Soupy Saturdays

And coming soon
Going, Going, Gone!

Other books by Judy Blume

The One in the Middle Is the Green Kangaroo
Freckle Juice

The Fudge books
Tales of a Fourth Grade Nothing
Otherwise Known as Sheila the Great
Superfudge
Fudge-a-Mania
Double Fudge

Blubber
Iggie's House
Starring Sally J. Freedman as Herself
Are You There, God? It's Me, Margaret
It's Not the End of the World
Then Again, Maybe I Won't
Deenie
Just as Long as We're Together
Here's to You, Rachel Robinson

For older readers
Tiger Eyes
Forever
Letters to Judy: What Kids Wish They Could Tell You

The Pain and the Great One

Cool Zone

Judy Blume

Illustrated by
Kate Pankhurst

MACMILLAN CHILDREN'S BOOKS

To Levi and Reed Cooper
Two Cool Guys

First published 2008 by Delacorte Press, an imprint of
Random House Children's Books, New York

This edition published 2008 by Macmillan Children's Books
a division of Macmillan Publishers Limited
20 New Wharf Road, London N1 9RR
Basingstoke and Oxford
Associated companies throughout the world

www.panmacmillan.com

ISBN 978-0-230-70027-7

Text copyright © P&G Trust 2008
Illustrations copyright © Kate Pankhurst 2008

The right of Judy Blume and Kate Pankhurst to be identified as the
author and illustrator of this work has been asserted by them in
accordance with the Copyright, Designs and Patents Act 1988.

All rights reserved. No part of this publication may be
reproduced, stored in or introduced into a retrieval system, or
transmitted, in any form or by any means (electronic, mechanical,
photocopying, recording or otherwise), without the prior written
permission of the publisher. Any person who does any unauthorized
act in relation to this publication may be liable to criminal
prosecution and civil claims for damages.

1 3 5 7 9 8 6 4 2

A CIP catalogue record for this book is available from
the British Library.

Printed and bound in the UK by CPI Mackays, Chatham ME5 8TD

This book is sold subject to the condition that it shall not,
by way of trade or otherwise, be lent, resold, hired out,
or otherwise circulated without the publisher's prior consent
in any form of binding or cover other than that in which
it is published and without a similar condition including this
condition being imposed on the subsequent purchaser.

Contents

Meet the Pain

My sister's name is Abigail. I call her *The Great One* because she thinks she's so great. She says, "I don't think it, I know it!" When she says that I laugh like crazy. Then she gets mad. It's fun to make her mad. Who cares if she's in third grade and I'm just in first? That doesn't make her faster. Or stronger. Or even smarter. I don't get why Mom and Dad act like she's so special. Sometimes I think they love her more than me.

Meet the Great One

My brother's name is Jacob but everyone calls him Jake. Everyone but me. I call him *The Pain* because that's what he is. He's a first-grade pain. And he will always be a pain — even if he lives to be a hundred. Even then, I'll be two years older than him. I'll still know more about everything. And I'll always know exactly what he's thinking. That's just the way it is. I don't get why Mom and Dad act like he's so special. Sometimes I think they love him more than me.

Fifty-Fifty

The Great One

The Pain has a loose tooth. He wiggles it all day long. Wiggle, wiggle, wiggle. You'd think it was the first loose tooth in the history of the world.

Today at the school bus stop he opened his mouth. "Look at this!" he called proudly. The tooth was hanging by a thread. I could have reminded him that by the time I was in first grade I'd already lost three teeth. But I didn't.

Instead, when we got on the school bus, I offered to finish the job for him.

But he shut his mouth and shook his head. "OK . . . fine," I told him. "But don't come crying to me if you swallow it."

Just as the bus pulled up to school the Pain yelled, "Look . . . it fell out!" And he held up his tooth. Everyone cheered.

When we got off the bus he tried to give it to me. "I don't want your yucky tooth," I told him.

"But I'll lose it," he cried.
"Not if you're careful."
"But I lose everything."
"Too bad."

"I'll give you half of whatever the Tooth Fairy brings," he said.

Hmmm . . . half of whatever the Tooth Fairy brings, I thought. *Since it's his first tooth, that could mean more loot than usual.*

"Come on, Abigail . . ." the Pain said,
shoving his tooth in my face.

"We split it fifty-fifty?" I asked.

"Is that half?"

"Yes," I told him. "Exactly half."

"OK," he said. "Deal." We shook on it. Then I took his tooth. The Pain gave me a silly smile. He looked like a mini-dragon with that gap between his teeth.

As soon as he walked away I started to worry. *What if I lose his tooth? Think how disappointed he'll be.*

All day at school I worried. During recess I wanted to jump rope with Kaylee. But I was too scared I'd lose the tooth. Kaylee told me to put it in my pocket. "What if it falls out?" I asked.

"Give it to me," she said. "I'll hold it while you jump."

In art class I drew pictures of teeth.

At lunch I kept the tooth next to my sandwich as if it was a piece of candy.

During science I checked it under the microscope. Ms Valdez was impressed. She thought it was *my* tooth. "It's my brother's,"

I explained. "His first. And I'm responsible for it."

Ms Valdez gave me an envelope. "Put it in here," she said. I dropped the tooth inside. Ms Valdez licked the flap and pressed it closed. Then I wrote on the front: "The Pain's Tooth. Handle With Care".

Finally the school day ended. It was the longest school day in the history of the world. On the bus going home the Pain

asked to have his tooth back. I was *so* glad
to give him the envelope. Now my worries
were over.

That night, after his bath, the Pain couldn't
find his tooth. He still had the envelope but
it was empty. "I took care of your tooth all
day at school!" I shouted. "I didn't let it out
of my sight for one minute. And now look
– you lose everything!"

"I told you, didn't I?"

So we started looking. We looked
everywhere. In his pockets. In his
underwear. In his lunch box. Even in his
ears, just in case. But there was no tooth.
"Why did you open the envelope?" I asked.

"Because Dylan wanted to see my tooth
up close."

"Well, maybe Dylan has your tooth,"
I said.

"No, because he passed it to Justin."

"OK, let's call Justin and see if he has it."

"But after Justin I let Miranda hold it," he told me. "And then Riley wanted to smell it. "And Kamu—"

"Stop!" I shouted, covering my ears.

So he stopped. "What'll I put under my pillow?" he asked in a small voice. Any second now he was going to cry.

"A note to the Tooth Fairy," I told him.

"Will she understand?"

"Maybe. But it will have to be a very good note."

"You write it," he said.

"Write it yourself. It's not my problem."

"Please," he begged. "I'm only in first grade."

Suddenly I remembered that I get half of whatever he gets. "OK, I'll write it."

"Make it good," he said.

So I wrote to the Tooth Fairy. I told her how the Greatest Sister in the History of the World watched over the Pain's tooth all day. I told her if she didn't believe the note she should look inside his mouth.

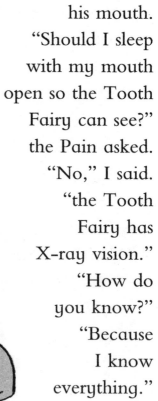

"Should I sleep with my mouth open so the Tooth Fairy can see?" the Pain asked.

"No," I said. "the Tooth Fairy has X-ray vision."

"How do you know?"

"Because I know everything."

I gave him one of my best *looks*. It's so easy to make him believe me. Then I shoved the note at him. "Sign your name."

"Not until you take out that line about the greatest sister in the history of the world."

"But I *am* the greatest sister in the history of the world."

"Who says?" he asked.

"Who says I'm not?"

"Abigail . . . Jake . . ." Mom called. "Time for bed."

The Pain printed his name at the bottom of the note. He put it under his pillow. Fluzzy jumped on to his bed and curled up in a ball. "Keep a lookout for the Tooth Fairy," I told Fluzzy.

Fluzzy yawned. What does he care about Tooth Fairies?

In the morning the note to the Tooth Fairy was gone and the Pain found a new dollar bill under his pillow. I was hoping for more, but a deal's a deal. So I reminded him, "Fifty-fifty."

He grabbed a pair of scissors, and before I could stop him he cut the dollar bill down the middle. "Fifty-fifty," he sang, handing me half.

I yelled so loud I scared Fluzzy. "You won't get away with this!"

Fluzzy jumped off the bed and hid in the closet. But the Pain just stood there smiling his dragon smile, holding his half of the loot.

The Soggy Egg Roll

The Pain

Grandma gave me a magnifying glass for my birthday. It comes from the science museum. It makes everything look twenty times bigger. "Watch this," I said to the Great One. I held the magnifying glass close to a dried leaf. When the sun came through, the leaf sizzled.

"Stop!" the Great One yelled. "That's dangerous."

I held up the leaf. My magnifying glass

is so strong it burned a hole right through it.

"Grandma never should have given you that magnifying glass," the Great One said. "You're way too young."

"Am not!"

"Are too!"

The next time Grandma came to visit, the Great One said, "I don't think Jake is old enough to have his own magnifying glass."

"I do," Grandma said. "He's interested in science."

"Ha ha," I said to the Great One. "*I'm* interested in science."

"*I'm* interested in science too," the Great One said. "Ms. Valdez is my favourite teacher and she teaches science."

"I'm glad to hear that," Grandma said.

"But no one ever gave *me* a magnifying glass from the science museum," the Great One told her.

"Did you ever ask for one?" Grandma said.

"No."

"Well, that explains it," Grandma said. "Now I know what you'd like for your next birthday."

That night the Great One came into the bathroom while I was brushing my teeth. "Did you *ask* for a magnifying glass for your birthday?" she said.

"Maybe," I said, spitting out toothpaste. I didn't have to tell her it was a surprise.

"It was a surprise, wasn't it?" the Great One said. "Admit it. You never asked for a magnifying glass."

"How did you know?" I said.

"I can read your mind," she told me.

"No, you can't!"

"Yes, I can! I always know what you're thinking."

The next day I took my magnifying glass to school for sharing. On the bus I showed it

19

to my friends Justin and Dylan. They looked
at each other's tongues through it. Then
they looked up each other's noses.

When the bus pulled up in front of school,
I stood to get off. That's when Roger Culley
grabbed my magnifying glass. That fifth-
grader grabbed it right out of my hand and
jumped off the bus with it!

I tugged at the Great One's sleeve.
"Roger Culley . . . Roger Culley . . ." I
couldn't get the words out.

"Roger Culley *what*?" the Great One
said.

Finally I cried, "Roger Culley stole my
magnifying glass!"

"What!" The Great One elbowed her
way to the door of the bus and flew out.
"Stop!" she shouted at Roger Culley. Roger
Culley is big. Roger Culley is mean. He
didn't stop.

The Great One chased him, yelling, "You can't do that to my brother! You give him back his magnifying glass right now." She leaped on to Roger's back. Roger fell to the ground. The Great One tried to wrestle the magnifying glass away from him.

Ms Valdez came out of school. "What's going on here?" she asked. She pulled the Great One off Roger. "Abigail Porter – I'm surprised at you!"

"But, Ms Valdez . . ." the Great One said, breathing hard. "Roger took my brother's magnifying glass."

Roger said, "I didn't take it. The kid gave it to me."

"Liar!" the Great One shouted.

"That's enough, Abigail," Ms Valdez said. She held out her hand. "Roger, give me the magnifying glass." Roger handed it to her. Then Ms Valdez looked at me. She said, "Jake . . . did you give Roger your magnifying glass?"

"No," I said, "I didn't give it to him. He took it."

Ms Valdez handed me my magnifying glass. Then she said, "Let's go, Roger." She marched him into school.

Roger turned and called over his shoulder, "You're *burnt toast*, Abigail!" Then he looked right at me. "You too – you little

crumb! You're both going to be sorry you messed with me."

"Roger!" Ms Valdez snapped. "Not another word."

I grabbed the Great One's arm. "I want to go home."

"And miss sharing because of that big bully?" she asked. "Come on, I'll walk you to your classroom."

I held on to her until I was safe inside room 101, with my teacher, Mary.

When it was time for sharing I was so excited I could hardly sit still. I almost forgot about Roger Culley. I couldn't wait until it was my turn. Finally Mary called on me.

I stood up and told my class that my magnifying glass is a real one, from the science museum. I explained how when the sun comes through the glass, it makes enough heat to sizzle a leaf.

Mary said, "Let's think of other things you can do with a magnifying glass, Jake."

So I told her you can use it the same way you'd use a microscope. "You can see things up close," I said. "Like little bugs, and toenails, and the hairs inside your nose."

"That's right," Mary said. "And you have to be old enough to use a real magnifying glass in a safe way."

Grandma thinks I'm old enough, I thought.

Then Mary asked if everyone could have a turn looking through my magnifying glass. I said, "Sure." So we stood around the science table and checked out rocks and sand and creatures.

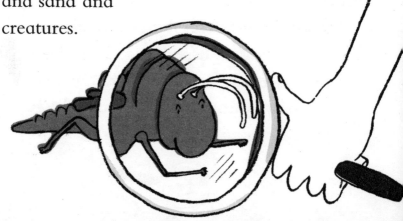

Mary thanked me for bringing it to school. She said she would keep it safe until the end of the day.

That afternoon Justin stuffed my magnifying glass into the bottom of his backpack. He shoved his jacket and a bunch of crumpled papers on top of it. That way it would be safe from Roger Culley on the bus.

But Roger wasn't on the bus.

At dinner the Great One told Mom and Dad how she saved me from Roger Culley. "That fifth-grade bully tried to steal from a first-grader."

"It was very brave of you to defend Jake," Dad said.

"Yes, it was," Mom said. "But . . ."

"But what?" the Great One asked.

"But sometimes the best way to deal

with a bully is to tell a grown-up you can trust," Mom said.

"Sometimes grown-ups don't do anything when you tell them," the Great One said.

"But Dad and I would always help," Mom said.

Dad nodded.

"I'll bet you wouldn't jump on the bully's back, like Abigail," I said. "You should have seen her. She ran so fast I thought she'd take off and fly. She could have been Superman's sister."

"Does Superman have a sister?" the Great One asked.

"I don't know," I told her. "But he should."

"Let's talk about what to do if this happens again," Mom said.

"It's not going to happen again," the

Great One said, "because I taught that bully a lesson."

"Honey . . ." Mom said to the Great One, "sometimes it's not that easy."

"Are you trying to scare me?" the Great One asked.

"No, of course not," Mom said. "I just want you to be prepared. There's nothing wrong with asking for help if you need it." She looked at Dad.

He nodded. "Mom is right. You can't always handle everything on your own."

"You'll remember that, won't you?" Mom asked the Great One.

The Great One nodded.

How come nobody said anything to me? It was *my* magnifying glass.

The next day at school, when the first-graders were on the playground, someone

27

tapped me on the shoulder. I thought it was one of my friends. But when I turned I got a big surprise – and not a good one. It was Roger Culley! "Hello, Jake," he said. Then he lifted me straight up and held me so my face was right up close to his. "You're *burnt toast*, just like your sister, unless I get that magnifying glass."

"Put me down!" I told him, trying not to sound scared.

"Or what?" he asked. Then he laughed and dropped me to the ground.

Justin and Dylan ran for Mrs Fisher, the teacher on playground duty. Mrs Fisher said, "What are you doing out of class, Roger?"

"I had to give Jake a message," Roger said. "See you later, Jakey!" he called, as if we were friends.

Mrs Fisher shook her head. "That boy . . ." she mumbled. But she didn't say anything else.

"Are you going to give him your magnifying glass?" Justin asked.

"No! My magnifying glass belongs to me."

On the bus going home from school I sat up front with Dylan, close to the bus driver. "My magnifying glass is safe at home,"

I said, "so what can Roger Culley do?"

"I don't know," Dylan said.

That was the problem. I didn't know either. And thinking about it made my stomach hurt.

But when Roger Culley got on the bus he passed right by without even looking at me.

"Phew . . ." Dylan said. "That was a close one."

I was glad it was the weekend. I didn't want to talk about Roger Culley. I didn't want to think about him either.

On Monday morning I sat with the Great One on the bus. She didn't tell me to go sit with my own friends like always. Instead she said, "What's wrong?"

"Nothing."

"Come on," she said. "Let's have it . . ."

"OK," I said. "What exactly does it mean when somebody says you're *burnt toast*?"

"You're still worrying about that bully?" she asked.

"Maybe."

"Don't listen to anything he says," she told me, "because he's worse than *burnt toast*."

"What's worse than *burnt toast*?"

She was quiet for a minute. I could tell she was thinking. Then she smiled. "A soggy egg roll," she said. "He's a soggy egg roll with chopped-up insides!"

I started to laugh. I laughed until Roger Culley got on the bus and sat in the seat right behind us. When he did, I moved closer to the Great One.

Roger leaned forward. I could feel his breath on the back of my neck. "Do you have anything for me, Jakey?" he asked.

"Get away from my brother," the Great One said.

I looked out the window and saw the sign that says SCHOOL ZONE. Someone had painted over the *s* and the *h* so now it said COOL ZONE. That sign meant we were almost there. And this time I was going to tell. I was going to tell about Roger. First I was going to tell my teacher. And later, after school, I was going to tell Mom and Dad. It made me feel better to think about what I was going to say.

But when the bus pulled into the school Roger leaned forward again. "I have a present for your sister," he said to me. "Something really special."

The Great One whipped around. "I don't want anything from you," she told Roger, "so you can keep your special present for yourself."

"But that would be a waste," Roger said.

When the door to the bus opened Roger shook a jar over the Great One's head. Then he ran off the bus.

We got off too. Three seconds later the Great One started screaming. She screamed and jumped up and down and slapped her head with her hands. "Help!" she cried. Her friends tried to help but they didn't know what was wrong until the Great One picked something out of her hair. She held it up for them to see. "Worms!" she cried. "He dumped worms on my head!"

Roger Culley laughed his head off while the Great One's friends helped pick the worms out of her hair. He was doubled over from laughing so hard.

Suddenly I felt more mad than scared, and I ran right at Roger. I wanted to jump on that *soggy egg roll* and smash

him. I wanted to scoop out his chopped-up insides and feed them to Horace, our class guinea pig. But when I got up close to the big bully I froze. I heard Mom's voice inside my head. *There's nothing wrong with asking for help if you need it.* And then I could hear Dad saying, *You can't always handle everything on your own.*

So I ran into school without looking back. I raced down the hallway. I didn't stop — not even when a teacher called, "No running in the halls!"

I ran until I got to the Great One's third-grade classroom. Her teacher, Mr Gee, was sitting at his desk. "The bully dumped worms on my sister's head!" I shouted. "My sister needs help!"

"What?!" Mr Gee jumped up and headed for the outside door.

But I kept running until I came to my classroom. I almost ran right into Mary. She caught me and said, "Jake, what's going on?"

At first I couldn't answer. I just kept gulping. When I could finally get the words

out, I told Mary everything. I told her how the bully scared me. I told her I was afraid to ride the school bus. I told her I was afraid in the playground. Mary said, "No one should have to be afraid at school. I'm glad you told me."

Before recess Mary read our class a story about a bully. Everyone got really quiet at first. We talked about why some kids are bullies. And what to do if a bully tries to scare you. Then we all asked questions at once.

That afternoon Mary walked me to the school bus. I got on and sat across from the Great One. When I looked out the window Mary waved to me. I waved back. That's when I saw Roger Culley. He was leaving school with a grown-up. The grown-up didn't look happy. And neither did Roger Culley. He was crying. I pulled on the Great One's sleeve and pointed out my window. She stood up for a better view. "Ha!" she said. "Now he even *looks* like a soggy egg roll."

★

That night, before I went to bed, I wrapped my magnifying glass in an old T-shirt. I put two rubber bands around it. Then I took it to the Great One's room.

"What's this?" she asked when I gave it to her.

"It's a surprise," I said.

"A surprise for me?"

"Yes. Open it."

She opened the package. "A magnifying glass! How did you know I've always wanted one?"

"I can read your mind," I told her.

"No, you can't!" she said.

"Can too!"

"OK, prove it," she said. "What am I thinking right this second?"

I didn't know what she was thinking. But I knew what I was thinking. *Why did I give her my magnifying glass? How can I get it*

back? And if I can't get it back, will Grandma give me another one?

The Great One just stood there looking at me. I could tell she was waiting for me to say something, something to prove I could read her mind. So I said, "Wait. I have it now! You're thinking that I can use the magnifying glass whenever I want to."

"I am not!"

"Yes, you are . . . yes, you are . . . yes, you are!" I said, dancing around her.

"I am not!" she said again. "And only a terrible, disgusting, awful person tries to take back a gift!"

"Did I say I'm trying to take it back?"

"You don't have to say it. I know that's what you're thinking." Then she put the magnifying glass into her desk drawer and covered it with a lot of stuff.

I just smiled, because now I knew where it was.

Chasing Lucas

The Great One

All the girls in my class like Lucas. On the playground we chase him. We don't stop until we catch him. Then we knock him down and sit on him. One time Sasha kissed him. Lucas wiped his face and said, "Yuck!" Sasha laughed so hard she had to use her inhaler.

Our teacher, Mr Gee, is always telling us to leave Lucas alone. "He doesn't want to be chased. He doesn't want to be kissed.

Find another game to play."

But chasing Lucas is the best game. Too bad Lucas doesn't know it. He should be glad we chase him. Doesn't he know that means we like him?

At dinner, the Pain said, "Why do you chase Lucas on the playground?"

"How do you know about that?" I asked.

The Pain didn't answer. He just shoved another forkful of plain pasta into his mouth. He only eats white food these days. I gave him my best look and asked my question again. "How do you know about Lucas?"

"Everybody knows," he said.

"Does Lucas like to be chased?" Mom asked.

"He pretends he doesn't," I said.

43

"Are you sure he's pretending?" Mom said.

"Of *course* he's pretending," I told her.

"She's not the only one who chases him," the Pain said.

"Why don't you mind your own business?" I said.

But did he listen? *No.* "All her friends chase him too" he said.

Then he
laughed with his
mouth full
of pasta, as
if he was
telling the
biggest joke.
As if he was giving
away top-secret
information.
"I know more,"
he said to Mom and
Dad. "Want to hear?"

"*Stop!*" I shouted. "You're ruining everything. Just like always. You are *such* a pain!"

I looked at Mom and tried to explain. "It's a game. If the Pain was in third grade he'd get it. But he's just a first-grade baby."

"I'm *not* a baby!" the Pain shouted.

"Then why are you acting like one?"
I asked.

"Children," Mom said, "no fighting at the dinner table."

"No biting either," Dad said. "Unless it's your food."

"Is that supposed to be a joke?" I asked.

"Yes, Abigail," Dad said. "That's supposed to be a joke."

The next morning, on the school bus, I told Emily, Sasha and Kaylee what the Pain said at the dinner table.

"Does he know we *like* Lucas?" Emily asked.

"No," I said. "At least, I don't *think* he does."

"Good," Sasha said.

As we got off the school bus we saw Lucas. Emily is way bigger than Lucas.

So she came up from behind and, before Lucas knew what was happening, Emily lifted him into the air.

"Put me down!" Lucas yelled.

"Not until you let Abigail kiss you," Emily said.

"No!" Lucas cried.

Wait! I thought. *Who says I want to kiss him? Did I say I wanted to kiss him? No! Thanks a lot, Emily.*

But Emily wouldn't let him go until he said, "OK, OK . . . Abigail can kiss me."

Emily put him down and held him still. "Now, Abigail!" she said. "Hurry." Lucas was squirming.

"No, thank you," I told Emily. "You can kiss him instead." I started to walk away.

"Wait!" Lucas called. "I'd rather have Abigail do it."

I stopped and turned. A group of third-graders gathered around us. Emily was still holding Lucas tight. She wasn't giving up until someone kissed him. *Poor Lucas!* I thought.

The other kids started singing—

"Lucas and Abigail sitting in a tree
K-i-s-s-i-n-g.
First comes love,
Then comes marriage,
Then comes Abigail with the baby carriage."

I hate, hate, hate that stupid song! I started to walk away again. Then I turned back for one second, just in time to see Madison Purdy kiss Lucas. Lucas wiped the kiss off his face and ran to catch up with me. "How come *you* didn't want to kiss me?" he asked.

I shrugged.

"I thought you liked me," he said.

"I like *chasing* you," I told him.

"Same thing."

"No, it's not."

That afternoon we had science with Ms Valdez. She told us to choose partners. Lucas chose me. All the girls looked at me and smiled. But I didn't want to be partners with Lucas. I wanted to be partners with one of the girls. I wasn't even nice to him. I blamed

him for getting the wrong answer to our problem. I called him a toad.

"And you're a frog," Lucas said.

"I am *not* a frog!" I told him. "And I read those Frog and Toad books in first grade."

At recess the girls chased Max instead of Lucas. I watched, but I didn't run. Max screamed when the girls caught him. When they knocked him down and sat on him

Max cried until snot came out of his nose.

Mr Gee was on playground duty. "What's going on here?" he asked.

"It's a game!" Emily sang.

"It doesn't look like a game Max wants to play," Mr Gee said.

"I'll play," Lucas said.

"We don't want to chase *you* any more," Emily told him.

"Why not?" Lucas asked.

"Because it's no fun now," Emily said.

Mr Gee shook his head and said, "This game is over."

"Why?" Kaylee asked.

"Because it's not a good game. Find a game that everyone wants to play."

As soon as Mr Gee moved away from us Lucas called, "Boys chase girls!" And suddenly all the boys were chasing us. We

ran and screamed and tried to keep them
away. Sasha tripped and skinned her knee.
The boys sat on her until she yelled, "I can't
breathe! Help! I can't breathe!"

"Her inhaler," I shouted. "Sasha needs
her inhaler!"

"No, I don't," Sasha said, sitting up.
"I'm fine, except for my knee."

Mr Gee blew his whistle. "Mr Gee's third-graders, over here — right now! No more recess until you can behave on the playground."

At dinner Mom looked at me and said, "I've been thinking about that game."

"What game?" I asked.

"The one where you chase Lucas."

"That game is *so* over," I told her. "We're never playing that game again."

Mom nodded. "I'm glad."

But the Pain couldn't leave it alone. "Abigail is marrying Lucas!" he announced. Then he laughed with a mouthful of mashed potato. Some of it flew out of his mouth and landed next to my plate.

"Ewww . . ." I said. "Disgusting!"

"Not as disgusting as marrying Lucas," the Pain sang.

"I am *not* marrying Lucas! Lucas is a toad."

He started humming *Abigail and Lucas sitting in a tree . . .*

"Stop!" I told him.

"Children," Dad said, "this discussion is over."

But the Pain kept laughing.

The next day when I saw Lucas, I decided to tell him I didn't like him any more. So I went right up to him and said, "Hey, Lucas, guess what?"

"What?" Lucas asked.

And then I couldn't say it. I couldn't say anything. I just stood there.

That's when Lucas said, "Guess what, Abigail?"

"What?"

"I don't like you any more."

So I said, "Same."

Then Lucas said, "Good. So, you want to be my partner in science?"

And I said, "OK."

Then we both laughed.

Just then the Pain and his class walked by. He saw me laughing with Lucas. "Look," he called, "*Frog and Toad Are Friends!*"

Bruno's Ear

The Pain

Tomorrow is Bring Your Pet to School Day in first grade. But Fluzzy can't go. He can't go because he's a real, live pet. "Sorry, Fluzz," I told him. "No real pets allowed."

We can bring pictures of real pets, or we can bring pretend pets. I'm going to bring Bruno. He's my stuffed elephant. Grandma gave him to me when I was born.

"Are you going to tell your class about

Bruno's ear?" the Great One asked.

"There's nothing to tell," I said.

"Ha!" the Great One said.

"I rub Fluzzy's ears too," I told her.

"But you don't *chew* on Fluzzy's ears, do you? You don't put Fluzzy's ears in your mouth and slobber all over them. At least, I hope you don't. That would be so gross!"

The Great One dangled a fake bug over Fluzzy's head. Fluzzy batted his paws at it.

"Why don't you ask Fluzzy?" I said. "Fluzzy always tells the truth." I looked at him. "Right, Fluzz? You always tell the truth, don't you?"

Fluzzy miaowed.

"Suppose the other kids laugh at you?" the Great One said.

"Why would they laugh?"

"Because Bruno is a stuffed animal. Because he's light blue."

"He's not blue."

"OK, so he's grey now," the Great One said. "But that's just because he's old."

"He's not old. He's the same age as me," I told her.

"That's old for a stuffed animal."

"Bruno's *not* old!"

"OK . . . Bruno's not old," the Great One said. "He's just worn out."

"He's *not* worn out. He's perfect!" I hate when she says bad things about Bruno.

The next morning I dried Bruno's ear with Mom's hairdryer so no one could say it was wet and slobbery. Then I put him in my backpack. Bruno didn't mind. He was excited to be going to school with me.

At school, everyone in my class was excited too.

Maggie brought a toy zebra. "This is my pet," she said. "His name is Ziggy."

Justin brought a huge poster of a gorilla.

Dylan brought a stuffed dinosaur. The dinosaur was as tall as he was.

Everyone was ready for Bring Your Pet to School Day. Everyone but our teacher, Mary. *Where* is *Mary?* I wondered. She's never been absent. She's never even been late.

Then the student teacher from the other first grade came into our class. "I'm Tracy," she said, "and I'm going to be your teacher this morning."

"Where's Mary?" we all asked at once.

"Mary had a toothache," Tracy told us. "She went to the dentist."

"But today is Bring Your Pet to School Day," Maggie cried. "Mary *has* to be here."

"And she will be," Tracy said. "As soon as the dentist fixes her up."

"Are you a *substitute* teacher?" Justin asked.

"Yes, I guess I am," Tracy said.

"We've never had a substitute," Dylan said.

"Don't worry," Tracy said. "Mary spoke to me on the phone and told me all about Bring Your Pet to School Day. So, let's get started. Who wants to go first?"

We forgot about raising our hands. We jumped up and down and called out, *"Me, me, me!"*

"First-graders . . ." Tracy said in her teacher voice. "One at a time, *please*."

That's when the door to our classroom opened and Lila came in with a dog. A real, live dog. A very big, real, live dog. "This is Baby," she said.

"Oh my!" Tracy said. "A real, live dog! Mary said *pretend* pets. She didn't say anything about real ones."

"I didn't know that," Lila said. "I guess I didn't hear the part about *pretend*."

Baby looked at our class and barked. She pulled on her leash.

Our class went wild. We shouted, "Baby . . . here, Baby!"

"Stop!" Lila said. I don't know if she was saying that to us or to her dog.

We jumped up and down and kept calling to Baby.

Baby jumped too, and this time she broke away from Lila.

She raced around our classroom, dragging her leash. She knocked over everything in her path. Dylan's dinosaur went flying. Marco jumped on to his table and started screaming. So did Maggie. "Help!" they yelled.

Maybe Baby thought they were playing a game. She tried to get up on the tables too. That made Maggie and Marco scream louder.

Then Baby headed for the creature table. "Stop her before she gets our guinea pig!" Justin cried.

We all started chasing Baby. Baby barked. Baby ran. She knocked over the big trash can. She barrelled into the basket of balls in the corner. She crashed into our block skyscraper and it came tumbling down.

Justin shouted, "She thinks she's King Kong!"

"She's a dog tornado!" Dylan called.

"Baby!" Lila shouted. "Come!"

But Baby didn't listen.

Tracy clapped her hands. But none of us paid attention.

Everyone was running around, trying to capture Baby. But Baby was faster than all of us put together. She raced by my table and, before I could stop her, she snatched

Bruno and carried him away in her mouth. "Help!" I cried. "Baby's got my elephant!"

That's when the door to our classroom opened and the first-grade teacher from next door asked, "Is everything all right in here, Tracy?"

"No!" Tracy answered as Baby tore out of our classroom with Bruno still in her mouth.

"Stop!" I shouted. But Baby raced down the hall. I raced after her. The rest of the class raced after me. Except for Maggie and Marco, who were still on top of their tables, screaming.

Baby ran in and out of every classroom with an open door. Books and pencils went flying. Kids screamed. Kids laughed. Teachers looked surprised. "Somebody stop her . . . please!" I cried. "She has my elephant!"

Baby flew down the hall into the school

65

office. She zipped behind
the counter and into the
principal's office. Mrs
Foxworth jumped up.
"What's this?" she asked.

"It's Bring Your Pet
to School Day!" Justin
shouted.

"Pretend pets," Tracy
tried to explain. "It's
supposed to be *pretend* pets only."

"I didn't hear the *pretend* part," Lila cried.

"Baby's got my elephant!" I shouted.

Baby tore out of the office and out the
door leading to the playground.

The Great One's class was having gym.
"Somebody stop that dog!" I yelled.

"Is that Bruno in the dog's mouth?" the
Great One called to me.

"Yes, it's Bruno!"

The third-graders started chasing Baby too.

Tracy cried, "This is a disaster! I'm never going to get a teaching job now!"

Suddenly Baby turned towards the third-graders and started shaking Bruno. She shook and shook and shook until Bruno's insides started flying out. Soon Bruno's fuzz blew around in the wind like snow.

"No!" I cried. "No!"

The third-graders made a circle around Baby. They clapped their hands and chanted, "Baby . . . Baby . . . Baby . . ." But Baby still didn't let go of Bruno.

The Great One ran forward. She stepped on Baby's leash. Baby looked at the Great One. The Great One looked at Baby. "Drop it!" she told the dog. "Drop that elephant right now!" And just like that, Baby dropped Bruno.

It got very quiet as I walked over and looked down at Bruno. He was flat. And one of his ears was hanging by a thread. He looked dead. I picked up what was left of Bruno and held him close to me. This was the saddest day of my life.

"Maybe it's time to say goodbye to Bruno," the Great One said very softly.

"Say goodbye?" I could hardly talk.

"What do you mean? Where would
Bruno go?"

"Into the closet with your other old
toys," the Great One said. She put an arm
around me.

"Bruno's *not* a toy!" I told her. "I'll never say goodbye to him."

"Mary's class . . . over here, please."

We turned. It was Mary. Some of our class ran to her side and hugged her.

Tracy was close to crying. "It just got so out of control," she told Mary.

"I can see that," Mary said.

Lila cried, "Baby's a very good dog. Really. She just got excited."

Mary said, "Tracy, would you please take Lila to the office so she can call and ask her mom or dad to come get Baby?"

"Is Baby's day at school over?" Lila said.

"Yes," Mary said, "Baby's day at school is over."

Baby lay down with her head on her paws and yawned.

Mary led our class back to our room. She put on quiet-time music. We rested our heads on our tables. I rested mine on flat Bruno. Mary sat down next to me. "You must feel very sad," she said.

"Elephants have no natural predators," I told her.

"I know."

We were both quiet for a minute. Then Mary said, "I have an idea."

"What idea?" I asked.

"The elephant hospital."

"What elephant hospital?"

"I know of one," Mary said. "Can you do without Bruno until the end of the school day?"

"Yes. But I need him before I go to sleep tonight."

"I understand," Mary said. "You'll have him back in plenty of time."

I handed Bruno to Mary. "You'll take good care of him?"

"Very good care," Mary said.

That night Lila and her mother came to the house. They brought me a new stuffed elephant. "We're so sorry," Lila's mother said. "Aren't we sorry, Lila?"

Lila hid behind her mother. She said, "And Baby is sorry too."

The new elephant was grey and stiff. Even though I didn't want it, I said thank you.

Later the Great One said, "I'll take that new elephant if you don't want it." So I gave it to her.

Then I got into bed with Bruno. Bruno's ear was stitched back on. You could see where his tummy had been sewn up. He was much fatter. But he still smelled the same. And his ear tasted just right.

Two Flowers

The Great One

I've been thinking about my name. I'm not sure Abigail is the right name for me. I don't feel like an Abigail any more. I don't look like one either. At least I don't think I do. I need a new name. *Could I be Charlotte? I wondered. Or Tiffany? Or maybe Emma Rose? Yes!* As soon as I said it I knew it was the name for me. *Hello, Emma Rose,* I said to myself in the mirror, just to see how it would feel. It felt good.

I sat at my desk and tried writing my new name. I wrote it with a purple marker. Purple is my favourite colour. *Emma Rose Porter.* I liked the way it looked. I drew a picture of a rose to go with my new name.

All my friends will be so jealous, I thought. *They have such ordinary names.* But then I started thinking of all the girls at school already named Emma. Emma Lewis in fifth grade. Emma Greenspan, in fourth. Emma Rinaldi and Emma Wong, in third. Too many Emmas. So I crossed out *Emma* with my purple marker, which gave me a new idea. Instead of Emma, I'll be Violet.

Violet Rose. The girl with two flower names.

I looked at myself in the mirror. "Hello, Violet Rose."

Perfect! I thought.

At dinner I said, "Guess what?" Then I waited until Mom and Dad looked at me. That's how I know they're listening.

"What?" Mom said.

"I've decided to change my name. From now on call me Violet Rose."

The Pain was drinking milk. He laughed when I said my new name – and when he did, milk sprayed out of his nose. "Ewww . . . that is *so* disgusting!" I made a face.

Dad passed him a napkin. But the Pain kept laughing.

"It's not funny!" I told him.

"Yes, it is!" he said.

Mom put down her fork and gave me a serious look. "Abigail is a beautiful name."

Dad nodded.

"We chose it just for you," Mom said.

Dad nodded again. Then he said, "We knew as soon as we held you, you were our little Abigail." He reached for Mom's hand.

"Kids should get to choose their own names," I told them. But they weren't looking at me any more.

I went to sleep dreaming of my new name and all the good things that will happen now that I'm Violet Rose.

The next morning I wrote my new name on my lunch bag. *Violet Rose.*

I decorated the bag with tiny rosebuds and a chain of violets.

At the bus stop I reminded the Pain to call me *Violet Rose*.

On the school bus I sat with Emily. Kaylee and Sasha sat across from us.

They were talking about Lucas. I waited for them to finish so I could tell them about my new name. For now, it was still my secret.

Suddenly a voice from the front of the bus called out, "Hey, Violet Rose . . ."

Everyone on the bus turned around. *Who is Violet Rose?* they wondered. *Is she a new girl? What grade is she in?* No one knew the answer except my blabbermouth

brother and me. I wanted to tell my friends when I was ready. But, as usual, the Pain ruined my plan. Just like he ruins everything! I wanted to tell him to shut up, but now it was too late.

When we got to school, the Pain said, "Hey, Violet Rose, you took my lunch bag."

"Did not," I said.

"Then what does this say?" He shoved his lunch bag in my face.

Uh-oh. I grabbed the bag that said *Violet Rose,* the bag I'd personally decorated.

I handed him the one that said *Jake.* "Why did you take *my* bag?" I asked.

"I didn't," he said. "You took mine."

Sasha looked at me. "Why is he calling you Violet Rose?" she asked.

The Pain was listening. So I whispered, "I'll tell you later."

The Pain followed me to my classroom. Before I could shoo him away he yelled as loud as he could, "Bye, Violet Rose. See you later."

"Shut up!" I hissed.

At recess the boys made a circle around me. They sang,

> "Violet Rose, Violet Rose,
> A stupid name
> That grows and grows
> From her nose
> To her toes.
> She's Violet Rose
> Wherever she goes!"

Then they laughed.

Emily pushed her way through the circle. She put her hands on her hips and glared at the boys. Nobody can glare better than Emily. The boys took off to kick around a soccer ball.

Then Emily said, "Is Violet Rose your real name?"

"No," I told her. "I made it up."

"Well, it's a beautiful name."

"Thank you."

"I wish my name could be Sierra."

"It can be," I told her.

By the time school was over, Sasha, Kaylee and Emily all had new names, just like me.

Emily was Sierra.

Sasha was Jamison.

Kaylee was Amber.

We told our teacher, Mr Gee, about our new names. He said he'd try to remember but he couldn't promise.

When I saw Ms Valdez, our science teacher, I said, "Have you heard? I've changed my name to Violet Rose."

Ms Valdez said, "Two flowers."

"Yes," I said, pleased that she'd noticed. "Two flowers."

That afternoon I had ballet class. Kaylee had tap. Her mom dropped us at Miss Graceful's dance studio. Her real name is Miss Grace, but we call her Miss Graceful when she's not listening.

I told Miss Graceful to call me Violet Rose.

"How am I supposed to remember that?" she asked.

"Think of two flowers," I said.

When we were at the barre Miss Graceful said, "Very nice, Rosebud."

I didn't even try to correct her.

Madison Purdy was behind me. She laughed. I don't like Madison Purdy.

In the ballet changing room after class Madison Purdy said, "So, Rosebud . . ."

"It's *Violet!*" I told her. "Not Rosebud."

"Anything is better than Abigail," she said. "Abigail is the most boring name ever."

"It is not!"

"Then why did you change it?" she asked.

"Who says I changed it?"

"I heard you tell Miss Graceful."

"That was just for today," I said, thinking fast. "It has to do with a play I'm in at . . . at . . . after school."

"Are you playing a flower?" Madison asked.

"Yes, a flower," I said.

"Are you sure you're not playing a weed?" Madison Purdy asked.

Everyone in the changing room laughed.

The next day after school we went to Emily's house. Her mom said, "Hello, Vicky."

Who is Vicky? I wondered.

Emily said, "Not *Vicky*, Mom. She's *Violet*."

"Violet *Rose*," I added. "The girl with two flower names."

Emily's mom smiled at me. There are four kids in Emily's family and her mom is always mixing up their names. Then Emily told her mom that from now on Sasha is *Jamison*, Kaylee is *Amber*, and she's *Sierra*.

"This is very hard," Emily's mom said. "It's making me tired."

It was making me tired too.

Later, when I got home, the Pain said, "What's wrong, Violet Rose?"

"Stop calling me that!" I told him.

"Calling you what?" he asked.

"You know what!"

"You mean Violet Rose?" he said.

"You *know* what I mean."

85

He started dancing around me, singing, *"Violet Rose, Violet Rose . . . grows . . . toes . . . nose . . . rows . . ."*

I shouted, "Stop!"

Charlie, our babysitter, ran in from the kitchen. She was getting dinner ready because Mom and Dad were both working late. Charlie is hopeless at cooking, so Mom leaves leftovers for her to heat up. "What's all that noise?" Charlie asked.

"It's Violet Rose," the Pain told her. "She's having a hissy fit."

"I'm very tired," I said. "I think I need a nap."

"A nap?" Charlie asked.

"Yes, a nap!"

I went up to my room, shut my door and flopped on my bed.

Later the phone rang. It was Sasha. "I've decided I don't want to be Jamison any more."

I was *so* glad to hear that. But before I could tell her how glad, she said, "From now on call me Lexi. And Kaylee says she wants to be Keesha. And Emily wants to be Rebecca. Isn't that cool?"

Now I had a headache.

"This is such a good idea!" Sasha said. "We're all so happy you thought of it."

But I wasn't so happy. I didn't think it was such a good idea at all.

The next morning, the Pain said, "How do you spell *Spidey*?"

"Spidey?"

"Yeah. It's short for Spider-Man. I'm changing my name too."

"Spider-Man is the name of an action hero," I said. "It's not a real name."

"So? I can be Spidey if I want. Just like you can be Violet Rose."

"Forget Violet Rose," I told him. "From now on call me Abigail."

"But I was just getting used to Violet Rose," he said. "I like the way you can rhyme *Rose* with *nose* and *toes* and *goes* and—"

"Stop!" I shouted.

"OK . . ."

"OK who?"

"OK . . . Abigail?"

"Right. And don't forget it."

He started singing, "*Abigail . . . Abigail . . . snail, fail, jail . . .*"

"No more rhymes!" I told him.

"But rhymes are fun," he said.

"Make rhymes with your own name."

"OK." He skipped out of the kitchen. I heard him singing, "*Spidey, didey, lydie, bydie . . .*"

I ran up to my room. I took one last look in my mirror. *Abigail,* I said to myself. Then I sat at my desk and wrote it in big letters with my purple marker. *Perfect,* I thought. *Totally, one hundred per cent perfect!*

The Breaf-kast Cafe

The Pain

My class is starting a restaurant. It will be open for one day. Everyone has a job. I'm going to be a waiter!

"Guess what our restaurant is called!" I asked the Great One. But I didn't wait for her to guess. "It's called the Breaf-kast Cafe,"

I told her. "Isn't that a good name?"

"You mean *breakfast*?"

"That's what I said."

"No, you put the *f* sound before the *k*."

I didn't answer. Who cares if I say it my own way? "Don't forget to call to make a reservation," I reminded Mom and Dad. "It's a family restaurant, and if you're lucky you'll get my table."

"Lucky?" the Great One mumbled.

"Abigail . . ." Mom said, in her voice that means *That's enough.*

Then Mom looked at me and smiled. "I've already called. I made a reservation for three people at eight thirty."

"What three people?" I asked.

Mom said, "Dad, Abigail and me."

"The Great One is coming to the Breafkast Cafe?"

"You just said it's a *family* restaurant," the Great One said. "And in case you forgot, I'm part of your family. I only hope there'll be something good to eat."

91

I didn't tell her all the good things there will be to eat. Let her be surprised.

She won't believe how much my class knows about restaurants. We even visited a restaurant. It was called Baci. Marco's dad is the chef. He wore a tall white hat. We watched him make pasta in the kitchen. He made it himself from flour and water. Not

from a box. I thought he was making the world's longest noodle.

Later we got to ask Marco's dad questions. I asked, "Do you ever make flops?"

"Flops?" Marco's dad said.

"Yes," I told him. "Flops. Like when my mom says, 'This dinner was a flop.'"

"Oh, you mean *mistakes*." Marco's dad said.

I nodded.

Marco's dad said, "We try not to make flops. But every now and then . . ."

Marco shouted, "Like that time there was too much salt in the soup!"

Marco's dad looked unhappy. He said, "But that only happened once. We learn from our flops!"

Then the waiters taught us how to take orders and serve the food.

The maître d' showed us the reservation book.

The manager told us her job is really hard. She has to worry about everything. Whenever something goes wrong, the manager has to fix it. I never want to be a manager.

After, we sat at a long table and had lunch.

I ate plain pasta. Plain pasta is my favourite food. No tomato sauce for me. My teacher says I'm going to turn into a noodle. If I do, I hope it's a really long noodle, like the one Marco's dad was making in the kitchen.

The night before the Breaf-kast Cafe opened I said, "I have to go to bed now. When you're a waiter at the Breaf-kast Cafe, you have to get a good night's sleep."

"It's not *breaf-kast*," the Great One said again. "It's *breakfast*. Why can't you get that right?"

I didn't answer.

"He never listens to me," the Great One complained to Mom and Dad. "Why doesn't he *ever* listen?"

I *do* listen. I just pretend that I don't. Waiters have to be good listeners. Tomorrow the Great One will find out what a good listener I really am.

95

That night I dreamed
I dropped ten plates of scrambled
eggs. The eggs flew through the
air and landed everywhere. In
Mom's shoes. Inside Dad's pants.
In the Great One's hair. Then
they turned into baby chicks.
The chicks ran around the
classroom. I tried to catch
them and stuff them in my

pockets. "You are going to be in so much trouble!" the Great One shouted. Then the police came. I hid under a table. They told my teacher it's against the law to have chicks at a restaurant. They closed down the Breaf-kast Cafe. They took my teacher to jail. Everyone blamed me. "Jake, Jake, Jake!" they shouted, trying to pull me out from under the table.

"Jake, Jake, Jake . . . wake up!"

I opened my eyes. It was morning. "Time to get up, honey," Mom said. "You don't want to be late today."

I jumped out of bed so fast I scared Fluzzy. Fluzzy likes to play in the morning. "Sorry, Fluzz," I told him, "but today is a special day!"

For once I got into the bathroom before the Great One. I remembered to brush my teeth without Mom reminding me. Waiters

need to have clean teeth. They have to smile at all the customers.

At school, our classroom was decorated to look like a restaurant. A big sign said WELCOME TO THE BREAKFAST CAFE. Every table had a bunch of flowers in the middle. The place mats were the ones we'd made.

When the bell rang, Mary called a class meeting in the hall. She said, "I know you're all going to do a great job!" Then she helped the waiters put on their long blue aprons. The chefs got to wear tall white hats. When I saw them I wondered if it would be more fun to be a chef. They don't have to write. They don't have to worry about spelling *cereal* wrong. Then I remembered I don't have to spell it. I can just write *C* for cereal. I felt better. As soon as my apron was tied I started jumping up and down.

Mary put her hand on my head. "Let's all take a deep breath. That will help us relax."

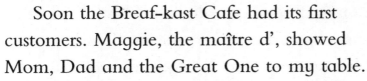

So we all took a deep breath.

"OK," Mary said. "Let's open for business."

Soon the Breaf-kast Cafe had its first customers. Maggie, the maître d', showed Mom, Dad and the Great One to my table.

"Good morning," I said when they were seated. "Welcome to the Br . . ." I started to say. But I didn't finish. I didn't want the Great One telling me I was saying it the wrong way again. Instead I skipped that part. "My name is Jake," I told them. "I'll be your waiter this morning."

"My name is Abigail," the Great One

said, as if I didn't know. "I'll be your
customer this morning. What do you have?
I'm starving."

I said, "We have scrambled eggs, juice,
water, coffee, bagels, muffins—"

"What kind of muffins?" Dad asked.

"Blueberry," I told him.

"OK," Dad said. "I'll have a blueberry muffin and coffee."

Mom ordered scrambled eggs and coffee.

The Great One pointed to the next table. "How come *that* person is having cereal?" she asked. "And how come *that* person is having fresh fruit? Don't you have a menu or something?"

Uh-oh! Maggie was supposed to hand out menus but she forgot. I spun around and ran across the room. But before I could get to the menus, I smashed into Riley. He was carrying two plates of scrambled eggs. *Crash!* Now the eggs were all over the floor.

Riley shouted, "Look what you did!"

"It was an accident," I told him. Any minute I thought the scrambled eggs would turn into chicks like in my dream.

I kneeled down to help Riley clean up

101

the mess, but he called, "Mary . . . Jake is trying to do *my* job!"

Mary came over to see what was going on. "Jake, you can get back to your table now."

"But Maggie forgot to give my customers menus."

"OK – give them menus," Mary said.

"Then get your order in. We're getting very busy."

I ran back to my table and handed the Great One a menu. She took her time reading it. Finally, she said, "I'll have cereal with banana. What kind do you have?"

"All the bananas are the same."

"I *mean,* what kind of cereal do you have?" she said.

"It's home-made," I told her. "The cereal chef makes it."

The Great One looked over at Lila, the cereal chef. Boxes of cereals were lined up in front of her. She mixed some from each box into a bowl.

"She's putting her hand into the cereal box!" the Great One announced to the whole room. "She's touching the cereal with her fingers. *Ewww . . .*"

"Abigail . . ." Mom said.

"What?"

"You *know* what."

But it was too late. Lila was already crying. "Now look," I said to the Great One. "You made Lila cry."

"Well, I'm sorry," the Great One said, "but I don't want her sticky little fingers in *my* cereal."

"Order something else," Mom told her.

"I'll have a bagel," the Great One said. "Make that a *toasted* bagel. With strawberry jam. And orange juice. I'll have a big glass of orange juice."

I wrote BT/J for bagel, toasted, with jam. I wrote OJ for orange juice. "Will that be it?" I asked.

"That's it," Dad said, looking at his watch.

I took my order to the kitchen. The kitchen was set up in the back of our classroom. Marco's dad was scrambling eggs.

He handed me a full plate. I carried it very carefully and set it down in front of Mom. "Eat while it's hot," I told her.

Then I brought everything else, including a big blob of strawberry jam for the Great One's bagel. "Will that be all?" I asked.

Dad said, "Yes, thank you. I think we have everything we need."

Then I stood there, watching them eat. "How's your food?" I asked.

"Very good," Mom said.

"Do you have to stand over us?" the Great One asked. "Don't you have another table to wait on?"

I looked around. The Breaf-kast Cafe was buzzing. Every table was full. There were no seats left except one, at my table. That's when Mrs Foxworth walked in. She's the school principal. That meant *I* was going to wait on the principal.

105

The Great One sat up straighter in her
chair when Mrs Foxworth sat down at
the table. "Hmmm . . . everything looks so
good," the principal said. "What do you
recommend?"

"The eggs are very good," Mom said.

"So is the blueberry muffin," Dad said.

Mrs. Foxworth thought it over. "OK. I'll have scrambled eggs, a muffin and orange juice."

I wrote that down. Then I jumped as high as I could and spun around.

"You're a little jumping bean, aren't you?" Mrs Foxworth said.

The Great One laughed. "I'd say he's more like a fava bean."

"I'm *not* a fava bean!" I said. I don't know what a fava bean is. I never even heard of a fava bean. But I know I'm not one. I'm not *any* kind of bean.

I wanted to step on the Great One's foot for calling me a fava bean. But her feet were under the table. Besides, I know the rules. No matter how much a waiter wants to step on a customer's foot – or even throw a plate of food in the customer's face – the customer is always right.

I went to get Mrs Foxworth's food. I was next in line for scrambled eggs when I heard a shriek from across the room. Everyone turned to see what was happening.

"There's a fly in my jam!" a voice called. I'd know that voice anywhere. I'd know it on another planet. I picked up my order of eggs and ran back to my table. I served Mrs Foxworth. Then I looked at the Great One's plate. There *was* a fly stuck in her strawberry jam.

I raced across the room to get Dylan because he's a manager. Managers have a really hard job. They have to fix all the problems. I grabbed his hand and dragged him back to my table. Then I pointed to my sister's plate. "What seems to be the problem?" Dylan asked the Great One. He sounded very grown up.

"The problem is, there's a fly in my jam!" the Great One told him.

Dylan looked at me. "The customer is always right," he said. "If the customer says there's a fly in her jam . . ."

"But there *is* a fly in her jam!" I told him.

"Waiter . . ." Dylan said, as if he didn't know my name, "take away that plate and bring the customer something else. Would you like another bagel?" he asked the Great One. "Why not try it with cream cheese this time?" He tried to snap his fingers but no sound came out. "Waiter . . . the customer will have a bagel with cream cheese."

"Don't forget to toast the bagel," the Great One called.

I took away the Great One's plate. I brought her one with cream cheese. Mrs Foxworth was finished eating by then.

She'd left half her blueberry muffin on her plate. "Can I bring you something else?" I asked her.

"No, thank you," she said. "I'm full." She patted her middle.

"Then can I have the rest of your muffin?"

The Great One gave a big hoot. "I thought you only eat white food."

"I'll pick out the blueberries," I said.

Mom said, "Jake!"

"What?"

Dad said, "Waiters don't eat leftover food off the customers' plates."

"But I'm hungry," I said.

"Well, of course you are!" Mrs Foxworth said. "You've been working hard. Your whole class has been working hard." She stood up and clapped her hands to get everyone's attention. The room grew quiet. "Boys and girls . . ." She smiled at all of us.

"This is a wonderful restaurant. You've done such a good job!" Then Dad started to clap and Mrs Foxworth clapped with him. All the other customers clapped too. Even the Great One clapped her hands!

"Now I've got to get back to work," Mrs Foxworth told us.

I said, "Thank you for coming to the Breakfast Cafe, Mrs Foxworth."

"The pleasure was all mine." Mrs Foxworth shook my hand.

"Did you hear that?" the Great One asked Mom and Dad. "Did you hear what he just said?"

Mom and Dad looked at each other. "Hear what?" Dad said.

"Jake said *breakfast*," the Great One told them. "He finally got it right. He put the *k* sound before the *f*."

"I did?"

"Yes, you did!" She held up her hand for a high five. I gave her a hard one. Then she said, "Now if only you would listen to me about everything . . . I could teach you *so* much!"

"Not as much as I could teach you!" I sang. And I started jumping up and down again.

Fluzzy Forever

I could teach *them* so much if only they
could read my mind.

They say they can.

They say they always
know what I'm thinking.

So how come they don't
know I need a new name?

I don't feel like a Fluzzy.

I don't look like a Fluzzy.

So from now on when they call *Fluzzy*,
I won't come.

Maybe then they'll get it.

Fluzzy . . . where are you?
Come on, Fluzzy. . . .
He's hiding.
He's probably under the bed.
Fluzzy . . . supper!

This is hard.
I'm hungry.
I want my supper.
But if I come out now
I'll never get a new name.

We have to get that cat a bell!
A bell – yes, that's a good idea.
A bell – then we'll always know where he is.
Tomorrow I'll get a bell for his collar.

A-bell! That must be my new name.
A-bell! I like it.

Soon the mom puts something
on my collar.
It makes music when I run.
It makes music when I groom.
It even makes music when I use my
litter box.

But now I can't hide from them.
I make music wherever I go.

A bell was such a good idea, they say.
He can't hide from us since he has a bell.
A bell really did the trick.

Yes, I'll show them that A-bell can
do tricks.

Watch this!

I jump
so high I
land on
top of the
bookcase.

Two
books fall
down.

That's a
good trick!

So how come at night when I'm on his
bed, he says,

Fluzzy, be quiet.
Fluzzy, stop moving.
Fluzzy, that bell is driving me crazy!

Does that mean they can't read my mind after all?

Does that mean they'll call me Fluzzy forever?

Oh, well – it could be worse.

My outside friend is called *Kitty*!

Acknowledgements

With many thanks to Mary Weaver and her first-grade
class for inspiring "The Breaf-kast Cafe"

and to

Leila Sachner for telling me the story of Lucy,
the inspiration for "Bruno's Ear".

A selected list of titles available from Macmillan Children's Books

The prices shown below are correct at the time of going to press. However, Macmillan Publishers reserves the right to show new retail prices on covers, which may differ from those previously advertised.

Judy Blume

The Pain and the Great One: Soupy Saturdays	978-0-230-70024-6	£7.99
Freckle Juice	978-0-330-30829-8	£3.99
Tales of a Fourth Grade Nothing	978-0-330-39817-6	£4.99
Otherwise Known as Sheila the Great	978-0-330-39814-5	£4.99
Superfudge	978-0-330-39816-9	£4.99
Fudge-a-Mania	978-0-330-39813-8	£4.99
Double Fudge	978-0-330-41354-1	£4.99

Audio editions

The Pain and the Great One: Soupy Saturdays	978-0-230-70663-7	£8.50
The Pain and the Great One: Cool Zone	978-0-230-70836-5	£8.50

All Pan Macmillan titles can be ordered from our website, www.panmacmillan.com, or from your local bookshop and are also available by post from:

Bookpost, PO Box 29, Douglas, Isle of Man IM99 1BQ

Credit cards accepted. For details:
Telephone: 01624 677237
Fax: 01624 670923
Email: bookshop@enterprise.net
www.bookpost.co.uk

Free postage and packing in the United Kingdom